Paddington and the Knickerbocker Rainbow

Michael Bond

illustrated by David McKee

Collins

One day Mr. Brown took Paddington and all the family to the sea-side for a treat. Paddington sat in the front of the car with Mr. and Mrs. Brown. Mrs. Bird, who looked after them, sat in the back with Jonathan and Judy.

But when they got to the sea-side it was
raining hard and there was a gale blowing.

"Some treat!" said Mrs. Bird, as she held
on to her hat.

"Look!" cried Paddington. "That man has had his hair blown away."

"Ssh!" hissed Judy. "He's bald."

But Paddington pulled his duffle coat up round his face. He didn't want his whiskers to blow away.

"Let's go in this café," said Mrs. Brown. "At least we shall be dry."

Paddington looked back at the sea. It was very rough.

"I think I shall put my arm bands on in case the tide comes in," he said.

As they sat down at a table, Mr. Brown pointed to a picture on the wall. It showed an ice-cream called a Knickerbocker Glory.

"If you can say that, Paddington," he said, "I'll buy you one as a treat."

Paddington was very excited at the thought and he tried several times to say it.

"Knickernocker Glory . . . Gickerlocker Kory . . . Lickerlocker Rory . . ." But the more he tried the harder it was.

"I think I may have a cornet instead, Mr. Brown," he said sadly. "It isn't easy saying 'Knickerbocker Glory'."

Everybody laughed. And because in the end
he had said it properly the girl brought him
an extra large one on a tray.

"I couldn't get any more into the glass,"
she said.

Paddington licked his lips. "What a nice nurse!" he exclaimed.

"That wasn't a nurse," said Judy. "That was a waitress. Nurses look after people who are ill."

"If Paddington eats all that," said Jonathan, "he'll need a nurse."

Paddington gave Jonathan a hard stare. "Bears are good at eating ice-cream," he said.

At that moment the sun came out. "I think it's going to be a nice day after all," said Mr. Brown. "Look – there's a rainbow."

"Quick, Paddington," said Mrs. Brown. "Look, before it goes away."

Paddington stared out of the window. He had never seen a rainbow before.

"It looks just like my Knickerbocker Glory," he said.

"And it disappears almost as quickly," said Mrs. Bird, as the rainbow began to fade.

"You must make a wish," said Judy, "before the rainbow goes."

"Then we can play on the beach," said Jonathan.

"I wish," said Paddington happily, "I wish I could have a Knickerbocker Rainbow every day of the week."